Mystery of the Turtle Snatcher

By Kyla Steinkraus

Illustrated by David Ouro

Rourke
Educational Media
rourkeeducationalmedia.com

www.rourkeeducationalmedia.com

Edited by: Keli Sipperley
Cover and Interior layout by: Renee Brady
Cover and Interior Illustrations by: David Ouro

Library of Congress PCN Data

Mystery of the Turtle Snatcher / Kyla Steinkraus
(Rourke's Mystery Chapter Books)
ISBN (hard cover)(alk. paper) 978-1-63430-380-4
ISBN (soft cover) 978-1-63430-480-1
ISBN (e-Book) 978-1-63430-575-4
Library of Congress Control Number: 2015933736

Printed in China, FACE Worldwide Limited,
Kowloon, Hong Kong

Dear Parents and Teachers:

With twists and turns and red herrings, readers will enjoy the challenge of Rourke's Mystery Chapter Books. This series set at Watson Elementary School builds a cast of characters that readers quickly feel connected to. Embedded in each mystery are experiences that readers encounter at home or school. Topics of friendship, family, and growing up are featured within each book.

Mysteries open many doors for young readers and turn them into lifelong readers because they can't wait to find out what happens next. Readers build comprehension strategies by searching out clues through close reading in order to solve the mystery.

This genre spreads across many areas of study including history, science, and math. Exploring these topics through mysteries is a great way to engage readers in another area of interest. Reading mysteries relies on looking for patterns and decoding clues that help in learning math skills.

Whether readers are reading the books independently or you are reading with them, engaging with them after they have read the book is still important. We've included several activities at the end of each book to make this both fun and educational.

Do you think you and your reader have what it takes to be a detective? Can you solve the mystery? Will you accept the challenge?

Rourke Educational Media

Table of Contents

Chapter One

Megan the Big Meanie

On the third day of the third month of the third grade, I handed out birthday invitations to all the kids in room 113. I made them myself with pink glitter glue, sparkles, and little squares of colored lace. We were going to have a fancy tea party with fancy ruffled dresses, tiny cakes and cookies, and white china cups that you can only drink from if your pinky finger is sticking out.

My name is Tulena Clarissa Warren the first, but Mom and everybody else call me Tully. Mom says I am a fashionista, which means I really, really like clothes. I love anything that is bright, sparkly, glittery, striped, polka dotted, lacy, or fluffy. Today I wore my furry pink vest over a green rainbow T-shirt with a jean skirt and blue leggings dotted with pink circles.

We had just come back to class after first recess.

Kids were still getting drinks from the drinking fountain and grabbing their English books out of their lockers. Our teacher, Miss Flores, was busy shuffling papers at her desk, so I knew we had a few minutes for visiting.

I handed the invitations to my four best friends: Lyra, Caleb, Rocket, and Alex. Our desks were bunched together in groups of five, and we were super lucky that we all got to sit together.

It was also a lucky thing because the five of us are the members of the Gumshoe Gang. Mr. Sleuth, the school secretary, gave us that nickname since we solve so many of the mysteries that occur at Watson Elementary. And let me tell you, there are a lot. A gumshoe is a detective who cracks cases, which was a good thing because there was no way I was ever going to put gum on my favorite pair of purple sneakers.

"Oh, thank you!" Lyra said when I gave her the invite. "Can I borrow one of your beautiful dresses?" Lyra was an amazing singer. She could sometimes be so loud you wanted to clap your hands over your ears, but she made up for it by

being a great friend.

"Of course, Lyra," I said.

"When is the party?" Caleb asked, squinting at the invitation. "These letters are so squiggly I can't even read it!" Caleb loved math, telling jokes, and being really messy.

"It's called cursive, silly. And the party is this Sunday. That's five days away."

"I'll ask my mom as soon as I get home," Alex said, pushing on his glasses. Alex was really smart and great at science.

"Will there be anything related to aliens there?" Rocket asked. "Like an alien spaceship piñata? Or a green Planet Moog cake?" Rocket's real name was Ronald Gonzaga, but everybody called him Rocket because he could beat almost anybody in a race. He was also just plain silly.

"No, Rocket. This is my birthday, not yours."

Even though this was an elegant dress-up party, I'd invited all the boys in the class too. It was true that lots of my friends were boys, plus Mom said everybody should be included.

And "everybody included" also meant Megan

the Big Meanie, even though Megan did not like
me at all and would probably rip up my invitation
as soon as she got home. I stared across the room
to where she was sitting, whispering and giggling
with her best friend, Emily.

"Do you want me to go with you?" Lyra asked.

I shook my head. "I can do this." I marched over
to Megan's desk. Megan had sleek blond hair that
fell to her chin. She always wore boring outfits like
button-up sweaters and khaki pants so smooth
her mother probably ironed them every morning.

"Hey!" I said.

"Hay is for horses," Megan said in a snotty way. She didn't know that I loved horses, so that was not a problem for me.

"Megan and I both lost one of our front tooths!" Emily said, pointing at the empty space in her mouth.

"It's teeth, not tooths." Megan rolled her eyes.

"This is for you." I held out the invitation.

Megan stared at me like I was one of Rocket's aliens. "What's that?"

"Please come to my ninth birthday party," I said sweetly, even though I didn't feel very sweet at all.

Megan squirted several drops of hand sanitizer onto her hands. She kept a little bottle on her desk for any occasion where she might have to touch a germ. She took my invitation with her fingertips, glanced at it, and smirked at Emily. "What kind of invitation is this? Did a monkey make this?"

My face got all hot. "I made them."

Megan sniffed. "Well, if your idea of a fancy dress-up party is as weird and tacky as the outfits you're always wearing, then no thanks. I mean, who wears pink, green, and blue all at the same time? That is, like, so last century."

I felt like I wanted to run back home to bed, bury myself under my blankets, and hide forever and ever. Tears stung my eyes, but I blinked them away so Megan wouldn't see. "Well, you don't have to come, then."

My fingers shook as I handed Emily her invitation.

"Thanks!" she said. Megan cleared her throat and elbowed Emily. Emily looked down at her desk. "I mean, no thanks."

Just then our teacher, Miss Flores, clapped her hands. "Back to your seats, class! It's time for language arts." Miss Flores had curly black hair, and her name meant flower in Spanish. If Megan's name meant something in Spanish, it was probably poison ivy.

I shuffled back to my desk and slumped in my seat. I was used to Megan being mean. That's why I always called her Megan the Big Meanie in my head. But today her words pounded in my ears. My heart felt like giant fingers were squeezing it. Were my clothes really weird and tacky? Did everybody else think so, too? Maybe I wasn't a fashionista after all. Maybe I was a big tacky dork.

Miss Flores pointed to the whiteboard, which had a bunch of sentences on it. "This morning, we are going to talk about good punctuation."

Caleb poked my arm. "That means not being late."

"No," Lyra whispered. "That's punctual. Punctuation is periods and commas and stuff."

Caleb made a face. "I knew that. I was just testing you."

"We are going to read each sentence together, and then you can help me figure out what important parts of the sentence are missing, okay?" Miss Flores read the first sentence out loud: *My dogs breath is so bad it knocks squirrels out of trees*

The whole class burst out laughing. At least, everybody except me. Miss Flores was great at making learning fun. But right now nothing seemed fun.

"What's missing here?" Miss Flores asked.

"A cat!" Xavier yelled.

"Well, the cat is next," Miss Flores said. "Look at this sentence: *My cat is so lazy I have to hire other cats to take naps for her.*

Everybody howled with laughter. Rocket fell right out of his seat.

Abby raised her hand. "What does the bunny do, Miss Flores? I have a bunny!"

"Can we write one for a parakeet?" Carys asked.

"And my box turtle!" Emily said, bouncing in her chair. "Like, 'My turtle is so slow he walks backward'!"

Miss Flores held up her hands. "Emily, that was fantastic. Yes, let's write one for each of our pets. But first, we need to do the assignment. Deal?"

"Deal!" everybody yelled.

Everybody except for me. I didn't feel happy or excited, and not just because I didn't have a pet to add to the list. I stared down at the pink circles on my leggings. Maybe turning nine meant it was time to make some changes. And the first thing I was going to do was fix my style problem.

Chapter Two

Turtle-napped!

On Wednesday morning, I dug through my whole entire closet searching for the right outfit to wear. Clothes flew through the air in every direction as I tossed out neon colored pants and tie-dyed shirts and glitter-covered skirts. Finally there was a mound of clothes on the floor almost as tall as my head.

"Oh, dear!" Mom said as she tried to come into my room. She peeked around the clothes mountain. "What on Earth is going on in here?"

"Just getting dressed!" I climbed over my clothes, slid down the other side to the floor, and showed Mom my plain white T-shirt and brown corduroy pants.

Mom frowned. "Um. You look . . . different."

"Whew. Just what I was going for," I said brightly. I gave Mom a hug as she handed me my

lunch box and a breakfast bar.

At school, Mrs. Holmes acted almost the same way. She was standing at the front door greeting students as they came in. Mrs. Holmes was so short she almost had to stand on tiptoe to reach the drinking fountain, but she made up for it by being the boss of the whole school. "Oh, Tully! You look so . . . normal!"

"Thank you!" I said.

Mrs. Holmes frowned. The principal was stylish too. She wore pretty sparkly pins and sometimes she wore a big frilly purple hat. "I'm not sure I mean that in a good way," she said.

I didn't have time to find out what she meant because just then the bell rang. Mrs. Holmes waved goodbye as I hurried down the hall to room 113.

Mostly I saw lots of kids looking at me, but nobody else said much about my new style. That was okay. I knew they were thinking good thoughts.

Several of my friends said they could come to my party, including Javier, Abby, Lyra, Xavier, and Alex. Caleb and Rocket had forgotten to ask their parents, which was typical. Megan and Emily made gagging noises whenever they walked by my desk, but I tried to ignore them.

On Wednesday mornings and Friday afternoons, we went upstairs to the library. The library was a huge room with thousands of books stacked on rows of shelves that went all the way up to the ceiling. The librarian, Mr. Hornswoggle, had to use a stepladder to reach the highest books. Mr. Hornswoggle really loved books. He also loved animals. Even though the library was technically not a classroom, he had more class pets than any of the other teachers.

As soon as we got to the library, we all ran over to say hello. The pets were lined up in glass cages beneath the windows. There was a black rat snake named Zake, a white fluffy hamster named Howard, and a gigantic tarantula called Fluffy. Let me tell you, even though he was hairy, that spider was definitely not fluffy. There also was CoCo the turtle. Sometimes when he opened his mouth, he looked like he was grinning at you.

At the beginning of third grade, Mr. Hornswoggle gave me the very important responsibility of being a Caretaker. After school on different days, students were in charge of feeding, watering, and cleaning the pets and their cages. My day was Friday. I was also the only third grade Caretaker. I admit I had maybe a little too much pride about that.

Mr. Hornswoggle rang a little bell on his desk. That meant it was time to pick out our books for the week and check them out. After that, Mr. Hornswoggle would read us a story or an article about an interesting topic —strange animals or amazing places like Egypt or the Himalayas.

I'd put a pet as my number one on the birthday wish list I gave to Mom, but I wasn't sure whether to ask for a parrot or a St. Bernard dog or a python or a ferret, so I used the Dewey Decimal System to find the animal section to do some research.

Mr. Hornswoggle found me as I was flipping through a book of exotic pets like monkeys and jungle cats. "Did you know it's legal to have a chimpanzee for a pet?" I asked him.

"But is it wise? You can have a skunk for a pet, but would you want to?"

"Great idea!" I said. "Do you think their stinkiness is overrated? I bet my mom would go for it if she knew you recommended it."

Mr. Hornswoggle coughed and patted around his vest pockets for his glasses. Only problem was they were on his face already. "Eh. I am quite sure that is not what I just said."

I pointed to my eyes and cleared my throat.

"Eh. Of course. Thank you, dear. Oh, I did wish to speak with you. I am leaving after lunch for a meeting, and I won't be back until tomorrow. I usually take care of the animals myself on Wednesdays, but I was hoping you might be able to fill in for me today, maybe after school?"

My heart did a little leap. "Of course, Mr. Hornswoggle! I'll just phone my mother from the office. I'm sure she won't mind."

She didn't, of course. Mom is great like that. After school, I hugged all of my friends goodbye, slung my backpack over my shoulder, and made my way to the library.

Right away I noticed Howard the hamster's lid was ajar. Howard was running in his metal wheel. He gave me a look, twitched his nose, and kept right on running. I fixed his lid, then I got the plastic container full of crickets to feed to Fluffy.

And that's when I realized that the aquarium's lid was ajar too. CoCo always spent his time swimming around his aquarium or laying on a rock under his UV sun lamp, which Mr. Hornswoggle called "basking." He had webbed feet for swimming and beautiful black, green, and white swirls all over his skin and shell that helped him blend in. Only I searched his whole enclosure, and he wasn't basking or blending in anywhere.

CoCo was gone.

Clues in the Library

My heart was beating like a million pounding horses were stuck inside me. Where in the world was CoCo? Could he have climbed out of his glass cage? I got down on the floor and crawled around, checking under the tables and the bookcases. All I got were little white hairs stuck all over the knees of my pants.

Someone must have stolen CoCo! But why? *First things first*, I told myself. A good detective knows that details are the key to solving a case. If CoCo was stolen, then the library was definitely a crime scene.

I quickly pulled my notebook out of my backpack. I was in charge of writing down all the notes for our cases, which was usually stuff like suspects, clues, motives, and alibis. The notebook had yellow polka-dots with REAL DETECTIVE

CLUES: PRIVATE: NO PEEKING scrawled in purple marker across the front and THAT MEANS YOU! printed at the bottom.

I examined the scene. I wrote down that both Howard and CoCo's lids had been removed. I walked all along the row of cages, looking for something out of place. Aha! At the end of the table next to Zake's cage was a paper towel. Sitting on top of the paper towel was a large hunk of cheddar cheese with a single bite taken out. A bite so perfect I could see all the teeth marks.

I drew a picture of the tables with the cages on them. I put an X where I'd found the cheese. Then I carefully lifted the hunk of cheese and placed it in a plastic baggie. I always kept at least a dozen plastic baggies in my backpack. A Gumshoe never knew when she might land a new case. And from the looks of things, this was gonna be a big one.

I finished giving food and water to Howard and Zake, then I glanced at the clock. Mom wasn't coming until 3:45 p.m. Alex would be in extended day right now. I still had 20 minutes to go see him and tell him about CoCo!

Extended day was held in the gym after school. There were tables for crafts, games, doing homework, and an area for basketball or dodgeball. Alex was at the crafts table, drawing some kind of weird science experiment. Javier was building a house with glued Popsicle sticks. Megan was at the game table with a couple of fifth graders. They were all painting their nails some boring shade of beige.

I slipped into the seat opposite Alex. "CoCo's gone."

Alex looked up and squinted at me. "What are you doing here?"

"Never mind that. CoCo's been turtle-napped."

"What? The turtle's taking a nap?"

"No! Like kidnapped! CoCo's gone!"

Javier gasped. "That's terrible!"

"I know." I quickly explained what I'd found.

"We need to tell Mr. Hornswoggle," Alex said, putting down his marker.

"He won't be back at school until tomorrow. I was hoping we could figure out something today."

"What if he climbed out of his cage?" Alex

asked.

Javier shook his head. "Turtles can't climb. Especially aquatic turtles."

I stared at Javier. "Hey, you know a bunch about animals, right?"

Javier shrugged. "Some, I guess. My parents own the pet shop Claws and Paws down at the Centerville mall."

"That's right! Then you can help us."

Javier got a look on his face like he was being cornered into something he wasn't sure he liked. "I guess I can try."

I whipped out my notebook. "What do you mean by aquatic turtle?"

"Aquatic turtles need to be in water most of the time, that's why their feet are webbed. Land turtles like to swim sometimes, but they spend a lot of time, well, on land."

"What kind of aquatic turtle is CoCo?"

Javier shrugged again. "I don't know. Some kind of map turtle. The pattern of white, black, and green lines and circles all over his carapace look like a map, but there are lots of different kinds of map turtles. And we don't have any as pretty as him at the pet store."

I wrinkled my nose. "What's a carapace?"

"His shell."

"What does he eat?" Alex asked.

"I know that one," I said. "Little floating turtle food sticks, plus snails, crickets, worms, and sometimes chopped up lettuce bits."

"Yum," Alex said.

Just then Megan pranced over, waving her hands and blowing on her fingernails. She inched around the crafts table as if even looking at the glue, markers, and paints would make them explode all over her clothes. "What's all the excitement over here?"

Alex was about to tell her, but I narrowed my eyes at him. I had just noticed something about Megan's black V-neck sweater. I reached over and plucked off a short white hair.

"Eww! What is that?" Megan squealed.

I held it between my fingertips with one hand and picked up one of the white hairs stuck to the knees of my own pants. I put them side by side.

"Viola! A match!"

Megan made a face like she'd just had a bite of a sour lemon. She tried to wipe the rest of the white hairs off of her sweater, only her fingernails were still wet so she could only use her palms. It wasn't working so well for her.

"Megan, do you know whose hairs these are?"

"They could be from anywhere!"

"But they aren't from anywhere. These hairs prove you were at the scene of the crime!"

Megan looked at me. "What are you even talking about?"

"You were in the library when you weren't supposed to be."

Megan's face looked panicky. "No, I wasn't."

"The matching hairs prove it!" I said triumphantly. "One hair is from your sweater, and the other came from the library carpet. And they're both from Howard the hamster!"

Javier's mouth fell open. "Wow. That's amazing."

Megan blew a puff of air out of her cheeks. "Okay, fine. I snuck into the library during lunch because I knew Mr. Hornswoggle wasn't in there to catch me. Are you happy now?"

I crossed my arms. "I am very happy, thank you very much. Now hand over CoCo."

Megan glared at me. "Again, what are you talking about?"

"You just said that you snuck into the library to steal CoCo!" Alex said.

"No, I did not. I snuck into the library to play with Howard." Megan sighed and looked around like she was about to get into big trouble if anyone overheard. "My parents don't let me have any pets. So once in a while I like to play with that silly hamster. Okay? You win."

Only I didn't win anything at all. Not with CoCo still turtled-napped. I sank back into my chair and sighed sadly. "That is terrible news."

"Was CoCo still in his aquarium when you were there during lunch?" Alex asked.

"Yes. He was lying on that rock like he was a rock himself. Honestly, what do you people see in that thing?" She turned and stalked off in a huff.

And just like that, one suspect was down

already, and we were no closer to solving the mystery of the turtle snatcher.

Chapter Four

Million Dollar Turtle

The next morning, we didn't have to wait until first recess to go see Mr. Hornswoggle in the library. Mr. Hornswoggle came to room 113 just as we were moving over to the learning rug to play the Favorite Things game.

"May I speak with Tully for a moment?" Mr. Hornswoggle asked Miss Flores.

I quickly whispered the situation in Miss Flores' ear. She gave the Gumshoe Gang a hall pass. "Make it quick!"

We stepped out into the hall with Mr. Hornswoggle. I told him all about yesterday.

"Oh, dear," he said. "This is distressing."

"We're going to get CoCo back," I said.

"We're on the case, sir," said Alex.

Mr. Hornswoggle pulled a handkerchief out of his pocket and patted his forehead. "I very much hope so. You see, CoCo is gravid, and so we must make sure the turtle returns to the nest in time."

I had no idea what he was talking about. Lyra and I raised our eyebrows at each other. "Huh?"

"CoCo is pregnant."

"What?" I nearly shouted. "But CoCo is a boy!"

Mr. Hornswoggle shrugged his shoulders. "Everyone says 'he' and so I don't correct them, but he is very much a she."

"But, but, who—" Lyra sputtered, covering her mouth with her hands. Then she whispered, "Who is CoCo's husband?"

Mr. Hornswoggle chuckled. "It is a strange fact about turtles, but some females can lay a clutch of eggs years after mating. CoCo used to have a mate, but he passed away quite a while ago."

"Holy moly!" Lyra said.

"Wow, Mr. Hornswoggle!" Caleb said. "You are like an empty well of knowledge!"

"He means that as a compliment," said Alex.

I pulled my notebook out of my back pocket. Today I was just wearing regular blue jeans and a white T-shirt, no diamonds or sparkles or anything. "Mr. Hornswoggle, do you have any idea who would want to snatch a turtle?"

"Eh. Well. Hmm." Mr. Hornswoggle took off his glasses and started polishing them with his vest. "CoCo is a Cagle's Map turtle, which is pretty rare. They are only found in a certain river in Texas. And she is a very beautiful turtle with all those green circles and spirals on her carapace."

"That means shell," I said proudly.

"Which reminds me," Caleb said. "How do turtles talk to each other? With their shell phones!"

Rocket and Lyra giggled.

"And what do you get when you cross a turtle and a porcupine?"

"I give up," Rocket said.

"A slowpoke!"

"Okay, ha ha," I said. "Back to the case. Would someone want CoCo because she's rare?"

Mr. Hornswoggle nodded. "Possibly. An adult Cagle's Map turtle could easily sell for more than two hundred dollars, depending on the market. Hatchlings could go for well over one hundred dollars each."

Wow. That was a lot of cold, hard cash. I could probably buy a whole pony with that kind of money. "And since CoCo's pregnant, she could make even more money for whoever stole her."

"Yeah," Rocket said. "Like a million dollars!"

"Not quite that much," Mr. Hornswoggle said. "But whatever the reason she was taken, we need to get her back quickly."

We all promised him that we would crack the case. After Mr. Hornswoggle returned to the library, the Gumshoe Gang huddled close.

"Who are the lead suspects?" Lyra whispered.

"Megan was a suspect," I said sadly. "But she's been cleared."

Alex frowned and pushed on his glasses. "Who would know enough about turtles to know that CoCo might be worth some money? Or that he is a she? Or even that she's pregnant?"

We all looked at each other for a long minute. Then I said what everybody was thinking. "Javier."

Turtle Maps

We had to wait until first recess to talk to Javier again. Outside, the wind was crisp and the edges of the leaves on the maple trees were tinted with orange and red. I didn't have my usual braids, and the wind whipped my hair in all directions.

"Ack!" Rocket yelled, throwing up his arms. "Your hair is like the tentacles of an attacking alien! Keep back!"

I rolled my eyes at him but he couldn't see my face through all that whirling hair. I had to hold it back with both hands.

Across the playground, Megan and Emily were sitting on one of the benches. Megan's hair was smooth and shiny as a helmet. I sighed. "Come on already. Let's talk to Javier."

We found Javier on the swings. "Hey guys," he said, but he didn't look that happy to see us.

Alex and Caleb sat in the swings on either side of him. "Can you help us out with our case?" Alex asked.

"Um, okay," Javier said.

"How long can turtles live?"

"Like 30 years sometimes."

"Cool. So, it would be neat for your pet shop to have a rare turtle for sale, right?"

Javier cleared his throat. He glanced at me and then looked down at his hands. "I guess so. But it's my parent's store, not mine. We have a lot of other animals too, like lizards and gerbils and kittens and stuff."

"What would you do with a million bucks?" Rocket asked.

Javier blinked. "I don't know. Buy a zoo, maybe? Why?"

"Just wondering," I said. I had to shove all my hair inside the hood of my sweatshirt before I could pull out my notebook. I wrote down my notes so far. Suspect: Javier. Motive: profit from sale of CoCo and her adorable baby turtles. Evidence: weird, nervous behavior, possibly

because of guilty conscience.

"Could you tell us everything you did yesterday from before lunch until you left extended day?" I asked.

Javier's face crumpled. "You think I took CoCo?"

I felt a prick of sympathy. But detectives must be tough to get the truth. "We need the facts."

Javier shook his head. "I went to the same classes as you did. You can ask Miss Flores. I never asked for a hall pass. After school, I walked to extended day with Alex. I was with him the whole time."

Alex nodded. "That is true."

"We'll check your alibi with Miss Flores."

"So can I go now?" Javier folded and unfolded his hands in his lap. He kicked at the dirt beneath his swing.

I narrowed my eyes at him. "If you didn't do it, then how come you're acting so strange?"

Javier's face flushed red all the way down to his neck. He gulped. "I'm not very good at keeping secrets."

"Who are you keeping a secret for?"

He finally looked up at me. "You."

"What??!" Alex, Lyra, and I all yelled at the same time. We were so shocked, we didn't even jinx each other.

"What are you talking about?" Caleb asked.

Javier took a deep breath, and then he said all in a rush, "I'm not supposed to tell that Tully's mother came into Claws and Paws to buy Tully a pet for her birthday. And I'm not supposed to tell that I helped her and it's going to be a—"

"Whoa!" Lyra held up her hands.

All of a sudden I felt like I could float around on the windy air. I was getting a real live pet of my own! Probably not a pony though. But still! "What is it?"

"No!" Lyra said, pinching my arm. "Don't tell her. She wants to be surprised."

"No I don't!"

"Well, anyway, that's why I've been so nervous," Javier admitted sheepishly. "Every time I talked to you, I was afraid I would blurt it out!"

"I don't mind if you blurt it out," I said. "How

about just a hint? Is it furry? Spiky? Feathery? Scaly? All of the above?"

"Don't tell her!" Alex warned.

Lyra pulled me away from Javier. "Thank you for your help!" she called over her shoulder. She whispered to me, "New rule: No talking to Javier until your birthday party, got it?"

I had to promise and pinky swear three times before Lyra let me go.

Then Miss Flores blew her whistle, so we headed back toward the school.

"What now?" Caleb asked. "I feel like we're grasping at the straw that broke the camel's back!"

"Me too," Alex said. "Are there any other suspects?"

I heaved a giant sigh. "No. And time is running out for poor CoCo and her babies."

"Is there anyone else who would want a turtle, like for a pet?" Caleb asked.

Alex wrinkled his nose, which made his glasses almost slide off. "Well, Emily already has a turtle, and so does Xavier. Abby has a bunny. Carys has that yellow talking parakeet she brought for show and tell last year. I think everybody else has regular pets, like cats and dogs and Guinea pigs."

"People have pigs for pets?" Rocket asked incredulously.

Alex laughed. "Well, I think that's possible. But Guinea pigs are little furry rodents. Kind of like hamsters."

Thinking of hamsters made me think of fluffy Howard with his cute pink nose. Which made me think of the library, and CoCo's empty aquarium. And then I smacked my own forehead. "Guys! We've been missing a critical piece of evidence!" I'd almost completely forgotten about the block of cheese with the bite marks in it, which had probably been left by the turtle snatcher. And maybe we could use it to catch him!

Chapter Six

Taking a Bite Out of Crime

When I woke up on Friday morning, it was pouring rain outside. The sky was so dark, I almost crawled back beneath my blankets. But I had too much to do today, including solving the turtle snatcher case and bringing CoCo home safely.

Mom came into my room as I was brushing out my hair. I was dressed in khaki pants and a black long sleeved shirt.

"Would you like braids today?"

I looked at myself in the mirror and shook my head. "Can I cut my hair shorter?"

"How short?"

I held my finger up to my chin. "Like this."

Mom actually swayed on her feet like she might faint. "Tulena Warren, what is going on with you? You want to cut off your beautiful hair, and you've stopped wearing your fun outfits. What's wrong?"

I kept my eyes staring at myself in the mirror instead of looking at Mom. I shut my mouth into a straight line. I didn't want to tell how my insides got all squeezed up when Megan made fun of me. I didn't want to tell how I'd decided I wasn't ever going to feel that way again.

"Nothing, Mom," I said, kissing her on the cheek. Not telling her the truth made my stomach feel like it was tied up like knotty shoelaces.

When the bus dropped me off at school, I pulled my raincoat's hood over my head and dashed through the rain. Mr. Sleuth held the front door open for me. Caleb was standing in the lobby, shaking out his wet hair.

"It's raining cats and dogs!" Mr. Sleuth said.

"Don't step in a poodle!" Caleb said. He and Mr. Sleuth cracked up.

Just then lightning zigzagged across the sky and thunder crashed so loud the sound vibrated in my ears.

"How shocking!" Caleb said, giggling.

"Come on," I grabbed his hand. "We have work to do."

Caleb laughed at his own jokes all the way back to room 113.

I didn't get a chance to bring out the cheese evidence until first recess. The rain was still pounding against the roof, so we went to the gym. Miss Flores started dodgeball, which is usually one of my favorite games. Part of being a detective was knowing when you had to be responsible and work. CoCo was counting on us.

The Gumshoe Gang sat in a circle on the stage, hidden behind the blue stage curtain. We passed around the hunk of cheese, examining the bite marks with my magnifying glass. "This is definitely the size of a kid's mouth," Alex said.

"Like a third grade mouth?" Lyra asked. "Or fourth or fifth grade? Or what about younger kids? I mean, even the kindergarteners have library time."

"My sister Ella's in kindergarten," Caleb said in a low, serious voice. "She would totally turtle-nap CoCo."

"Have you seen a turtle at your house?" Alex asked.

"Nope."

I rolled my eyes up toward the ceiling. "Then it's probably not her."

"Who eats a big bar of cheese like this anyway?" Alex made a face.

"I would!" Caleb said.

Rocket held out his hands. "I would eat that right now if Tully would let me."

I pushed his hands away. "You don't get to touch the cheese."

"Look at these marks," Lyra said, examining the evidence with the magnifying glass. "You can see the marks of the top and bottom teeth biting all the way through the cheese, except for right there, in the front."

I leaped to my feet. "You're a genius! Whoever took that bite of cheese is missing a front tooth!"

"Megan and Emily are both missing teeth," Alex said, frowning. "But that doesn't make sense, because Megan has been cleared, and Emily already has a turtle. Why would she steal one?"

I sank back down. "I have no idea."

"We could still talk to Emily," Caleb said,

patting my shoulder. "Let's rattle her feathers!"

"The problem is she's always stuck like glue to Megan," I grumbled.

Alex nodded. "Let's try to find a way to talk to her alone."

"And during lunch we should make every kid in the whole school smile at us!" Rocket said.

"That's a good idea, Rocket," Alex said. "But I don't know if Mrs. Holmes would let us make suspects of every single student, especially the little ones."

"But it's the little ones who are the sneakiest," Caleb said with a grin. "Speaking from experience."

Chapter Seven

Rescuing CoCo

After language arts, lunch, and music, we finally had library time. Rain splashed the window panes, but the library was warm and bright and smelled wonderful, like dusty old books.

My stomach felt all sick and wiggly when I had to tell Mr. Hornswoggle we hadn't figured the case out yet. He wiped his face with his handkerchief and smiled sadly. "Well. Let's not give up just yet, then."

"We won't."

The rest of the class had spread out among the rows of bookshelves, searching for books to check out. "This might be a good time to find Emily," Alex said quietly.

We checked each row until we saw her. She was looking down at a book in her hand, standing in front of the same animals section I had searched

50

through on Wednesday. "Emily," I whispered.

She snapped the book shut and held it behind her back. "Hey, guys."

"Can we talk to you?" Alex asked.

Emily looked around, probably hoping Megan might save her. "Um, sure."

"We're looking for the turtle snatcher," I said, explaining about the cheese we found at the crime scene. "Whoever bit the cheese is missing a tooth, and so are you."

"That could be lots of people."

"Not as many as you might expect," Alex said.

library at all on Tuesday afternoon."

"No. Nope. Not me."

"It's important we find CoCo," I said. "She's pregnant and needs a safe place to lay her eggs."

Emily's face went a little white. "Really?" she squeaked. "I thought CoCo was a boy."

"Surprise!" Caleb said.

"Well, I don't think I can help you."

I was getting one of those funny detective feelings in my belly. "Emily, maybe you can help us. Can we see the book you were looking at?"

Emily hesitated, biting her lower lip. "Okay. It's just, you know, a turtle book, because I have a turtle already. As a pet, at home."

She handed me the book: *The Care and Feeding of Aquatic Turtles*.

I stared at the cover. I thought about all the details I'd written down in my notebook during my conversations with Javier and Mr. Hornswoggle. "Emily, isn't your turtle a box turtle?"

"Yes."

"Box turtles are land turtles, right?"

"Yes," Emily said so softly that I could barely

hear her.

"But this book is for taking care of an aquatic turtle—a water turtle. CoCo is an aquatic turtle."

Emily nodded. Her lower lip was trembling.

"Emily," I said gently. "Is there something you want to tell us?"

Emily started to cry. "I'm sorry. I took CoCo. It was me."

"But why?" Caleb asked.

Emily sniffed. "Because my turtle ran away. On Tuesday, I took Bubbles out to play in my backyard, so he could have some fun in the sunshine. I thought he was taking a nap so I went inside for a drink of water. I guess turtles can move really fast when they want to, because when I came back outside, he was gone. I looked everywhere. I knew I'd get in big trouble when my parents found out. And I missed Bubbles so much. I'm very sorry. I felt terrible this whole time."

"When did you do it?" Alex asked.

"When I heard Mr. Hornswoggle was going to be away from the library all afternoon on Wednesday, I thought it was the answer to all of my troubles. I sneaked away during lunch, taking my cheese stick with me to snack on. I was putting CoCo in my backpack when I heard a noise, so I crept behind one of the bookcases. Megan came in to play with Howard. As soon as she left, I ran right out of there. And that's it. Except CoCo is acting funny. He—I mean she—is not eating the food I'm giving her. She seems really unhappy."

I pointed to the book. "That's because land turtles and aquatic turtles are different. They eat different foods and aquatic turtles need lots of water to swim in. Plus, she might be getting ready to lay her eggs."

Emily rubbed her eyes with her sleeve. "I just want CoCo to be okay."

Lyra put her arm around Emily's shoulder. "We'll walk with you to see Mrs. Holmes."

Birthday Surprise

We went with Emily to Mrs. Holmes' office and explained everything. Mrs. Holmes called Emily's parents, who said they'd bring CoCo back by the end of the school day. Mrs. Holmes congratulated us on solving the case, and for our reward, she sent us right back to class.

But first, Mrs. Holmes pulled me aside. "Can I speak with you for a minute, Tully?"

My heart felt like it was jumping rope. "Okay," I whispered.

Mrs. Holmes sat down and folded her arms on her desk. "Can we talk about your outfit?"

I looked down. "Is there something wrong?"

Mrs. Holmes shook her head. "No dear, except for the fact that it isn't you. I happen to know that you have an exceptional fashion sense. I enjoy seeing you so colorful and sparkling every day."

I wrinkled my nose. "Really?"

"Oh yes I do. And I am not the only one. Now, I'm going to take a little guess that someone said something not very nice about your clothes."

I folded my hands in my lap. "Yes, ma'am."

"I also don't think I'd need to guess too hard to figure out who that might be." Mrs. Holmes said. "I could have a chat with this girl, but I think you

could probably do a better job."

"What do you mean?"

"When you are true to yourself and confident in who you are, that tends to scare off most of the bullies. Many times people are mean because they don't like themselves much. It makes them feel better to make you not like yourself either."

Wow. I'd never thought about it like that. I looked at my boring shirt. "I do miss my old clothes."

"Your fun fashion is something that makes you special. Just like CoCo. She has amazing green swirls and circles that make her quite beautiful. Anyway, I hope you think about that." Mrs. Holmes winked at me. She was pretty cool lady for someone who had to be the boss of the whole school.

******

My ninth birthday party was super fantastic. I wore my silver and pink striped knee socks, a puffy orange skirt, a neon yellow shirt with a green glitter unicorn on it, and a pink feather boa wrapped around my neck. All my friends came, and guess what? Megan the not-so-big Meanie showed up too. I think I even saw her smile once.

It turned out my birthday present from Mom was a giant glass aquarium with a note inside from Mr. Hornswoggle. When CoCo's hatchings get big enough, I will have two Cagle Map turtles for my very own. And THAT is a pretty good deal.

How to Solve a Mystery:
A Peek Inside Tully's Notebook

Suspect List: Megan, Javier, Emily

Megan's motive: General meanness

Evidence: White hairs prove she was at the scene of the crime!

Javier's motive: Family owns Paws and Claws, sell CoCo and make millions???

Evidence: Weird and nervous behavior.

Emily: No known motive.

Evidence: Missing front tooth matches crime scene cheese bite marks.

Q & A with Author Kyla Steinkraus

How did you come up with the idea for Mystery of the Turtle Snatcher?
I gave a talk at my son's school about the writing process. One of the students came up to me and suggested I write a mystery about a classroom pet turtle who suddenly goes missing. She already had the name of CoCo. I built the rest of the story around that idea.

Did you have any class pets when you were a student?
My third grade class pet was a giant tarantula just like Fluffy. Many students picked him up and let him crawl on their arms. I could never do that!

Do you have any pets now?
Yes, I have a big fat cat named Charlie Brown. He is quite lazy. He likes to snuggle next to my feet when I am writing.

Discussion Questions

1. Why did Tully stop wearing her colorful, fun outfits?
2. How did the clue of the bite mark in the cheese help Tully solve the case?
3. What is one difference between an aquatic turtle and a land turtle?
4. Do you think Emily felt happy after she stole CoCo? Why or why not?
5. Tully learned that her sense of style was part of what made her unique and special. What makes you unique and special?

Writing Prompt

What might happen if your class pet suddenly disappeared? What clues would the culprit leave behind? Who would you suspect? How would you solve the case?

Vocabulary

Write these words on index cards. Then shuffle them up and place them face down. Draw three cards at a time, then write a sentence that uses all three words. It might get tricky, so be creative!

aquatic   hesitate

bask   pluck

carapace   sleek

distress   snatch

examine

Websites to Visit

turtlepuddle.org/kidspage/questions.html

pacerkidsagainstbullying.org/kab/what-is-bullying

kids.mysterynet.com

About the Author

Kyla Steinkraus loves mysteries and third graders (she happens to have one at home), so writing books for this series was a perfect fit. She and her two awesome kids love to snuggle up and read good books together. Kyla also loves playing games, laughing at funny jokes, and eating anything with chocolate in it.

About the Illustrator

I have always loved drawing from a very young age. While I was at school, most of my time was spent drawing comics and copying my favorite characters. With a portfolio under my arm, I started drawing comics for newspapers and fanzines. After I finished my studies I decided to try and make a living as a freelance illustrator... and here I am!